Copyright © 2004 by Tony Ross
The rights of Tony Ross to be identified as the author and illustrator of this work
have been asserted by him in accordance with the Copyright, Designs and Patents Act, 1988.
First published in Great Britain in 2004 by Andersen Press Ltd, 20 Vauxhall Bridge Road,
London SW1V 2SA. Published in Australia by Random House Australia Pty.,
20 Alfred Street, Milsons Point, Sydney, NSW 2061. All rights reserved.
Colour separated in Switzerland by Photolitho AG, Zürich.
Printed and bound in Italy by Grafiche AZ, Verona.

10   9   8   7   6   5   4   3   2   1

British Library Cataloguing in Publication Data available.

ISBN 1 84270 296 3

This book has been printed on acid-free paper

Is it Because?

Ⓐ
Andersen Press
London

Pépé, is it because . . .

. . . is it because
he's got silly names?

Is it because
he's no good at games?

Is it because
he's friendless, you see?

Is it because
he lives in a tree?

Is it because
of the size of his head?

Is it because
he wees in his bed?

Is it because
he hasn't a dog?

Is it because
he's as thick as a log?

Is it because
he eats like a pig?

Is it because
his nose is so big?

Is it because
he misses his mum?

Is it because
he still sucks his thumb?

Is it because
he smells like a pike?

Is it because
he can't ride a bike?

Is it because
he's scared of the night?

Is it because
his pants are too tight?

Is it because
he's feeling so low?

Is it because . . . ?
Oh, I'll never know . . .

. . . why Peregrine Ffrogg
has to bully me so.

Perhaps it's because . . .
– I think I can see –

. . . perhaps it's because
he'd rather be me!